Love
Nanna
albina 1991

When Alice first saw the White Rabbit and followed him down the big rabbit-hole, it was the start of the most wonderful adventure a little girl could have.

Just imagine finding yourself having a conversation with a Blue Caterpillar on top of a mushroom. Or sitting down to tea with a March Hare, a Mad Hatter and a very gentle little Dormouse!

Of course there were times when Alice wasn't quite sure if she was really enjoying herself. It certainly wasn't much fun listening to the tearful Mock Turtle telling her his sad story. And it wasn't much fun being the guest of the Queen of Hearts. "Off with his head!" or "Off with her head!" was the terrible Queen's favorite command when any of the players at her Croquet Party upset her. No wonder Alice was glad to make her escape!

Lewis Carroll's

# ALICE in WONDERLAND

adapted by Jane Carruth
*illustrated by Rene Cloke*

**DERRYDALE**
**New York**

This 1990 edition published by Derrydale Books,
distributed by Outlet Book Company, Inc., a Random
House Company, 225 Park Avenue South, New York,
New York 10003

Printed and bound in Malaysia

ISBN 0–517–051915

87654321

# CONTENTS

## Chapter 1

# DOWN THE RABBIT-HOLE

Alice was beginning to feel very tired of sitting beside her sister on the bank with absolutely nothing to do. It was a hot day and the sun was making her very stupid and sleepy when suddenly a White Rabbit with pink eyes ran close by her. Alice didn't find that very strange but when the Rabbit actually took a watch out of its pocket and murmured, "Oh dear! I shall be too late!" Well – that was a different story and she jumped to her feet and ran after it across the field.

Fortunately, Alice was just in time to see the Rabbit pop down a big rabbit-hole.

In another moment Alice followed the Rabbit. It was just like falling down a very deep well. But the strange thing was she was falling so slowly that she had plenty of time to notice the maps and pictures and all kinds of books, jugs and bottles. Down, down, down she went until suddenly, thump, thump! she landed on a heap of dry leaves. The fall was over!

To her great relief the White Rabbit was still in

sight and Alice hurried after it. She was just in time to hear it murmur,

"Oh my ears and whiskers, how late it's getting," before it turned a corner and disappeared. Alice was now in a long hall.

All the doors round the hall were locked. But on a glass table she spied a tiny golden key. To her delight the key opened the smallest of the doors, and she knelt down and looked into a lovely garden.

It was the loveliest garden you ever saw and Alice longed to be walking in it. But she couldn't even push her head through the doorway. "And even if I could," she told herself sadly, "my head would be of little use without the rest of me!"

There didn't seem much point waiting beside the door so she went back to the table. There, to her surprise, she saw a little bottle which had certainly not been there before. Around its neck was a label with the words DRINK ME printed on it.

"I might as well," said Alice. The mixture inside was really very nice for it tasted of custard, cherry pie, toffee, and hot buttered toast.

Alice finished it. Then something very curious happened. She began growing smaller and smaller. "Now I'm just about the right size to get into that lovely garden," she told herself as soon as she felt she had stopped shrinking. Alas, poor Alice! No matter how hard she tried she could not climb the slippery table-leg to reach the golden key that lay on the glass table, and she began to cry.

# Chapter 2

## POOL OF TEARS

"It's no use crying," Alice told herself sharply. She took a deep breath and noticed for the first time a tiny piece of cake with the words EAT ME on it. "I might as well," said Alice.

Poor Alice! She had no sooner finished the cake than she found herself shooting upward until her head struck against the roof and she began to cry again. After a time she heard the patter of little feet and along trotted the White Rabbit. At the sight of her he dropped his gloves and fan.

To her dismay the Rabbit scurried away as fast as he could. Alice picked up the fan and white kid gloves and began fanning herself. "Dear! dear! How queer everything is today," she said aloud, having made up her mind to stop crying. "I don't feel ME any more. I wonder if I'm somebody else after all . . . And I'm

tired of being all alone in this hall and sitting in my own pool of tears. I really am!"

While she was talking she glanced down at her hands and was surprised to find she had put on the Rabbit's little white gloves. "I must be growing small again!" she exclaimed. "It must be the fan!" And she dropped it quickly. Then she began to wonder all over again if she really was Alice. "I'll try reciting some of my favorite verses just to see . . ." she decided.

*"How doth the little crocodile
 Improve his shining tail,
And pour the waters of the Nile
 On every golden scale!*

*How cheerfully he seems to grin,
 How neatly spread his claws,
And welcomes little fishes in
 With gently smiling jaws!"*

Alice tried saying the verses sitting down. Then she tried again standing up though it didn't seem to make much difference.

"I'm sure those are not the right words," she said and her eyes filled with tears. As she said this her foot slipped and in a moment she had fallen into her own pool of tears. Just then she heard something splashing about and there was a mouse that had slipped into the water, just like herself, coming towards her.

"Should I try speaking to this Mouse," Alice asked herself. "I'll try . . ."

The Mouse looked at her inquisitively and seemed to wink one of its little eyes, but it said nothing.

So she began, "O Mouse – do you know the way out of this pool?"

When the Mouse stayed silent, Alice decided to try again. "Perhaps it is a French Mouse after all," she thought.

So she began, "Où est ma chatte?" which was all she could say in French.

The Mouse gave a sudden leap out of the water, and seemed to quiver all over with fright.

"It must be a French Mouse," Alice told herself, watching it swim away at great speed. "That's how it knew 'chatte' meant 'cat' – oh dear!"

The pool was now getting very crowded with all

the birds and animals that had fallen into it; there was a Duck and a Dodo, a Lory and an Eaglet, and several other curious creatures. "I do think we should all make for the shore," Alice cried. "I'll lead the way and all of you follow me!"

# Chapter 3
## A CAUCUS-RACE

What a funny looking party they were when at last they were on the bank! The birds had sad-looking feathers and some of the animals had their fur clinging close to them. They were all dripping wet, cross and uncomfortable. Alice herself was not happy as she sat looking at them. But when she found herself talking to them it was as if she had known them all her life and she said as much!

"If you ask me," said Alice, after a short silence, "the most important thing is to do something to make us dry . . ."

"I know the very best thing to get us dry," said the Dodo suddenly. "It simply can't fail . . ."

"What?" asked the Eaglet. "Tell us!"

"It's a Caucus-race," said the Dodo.

"What is a Caucus-race?" Alice asked, not really wanting to know.

"The best way to explain is to do it," said the Dodo. "I'll begin by marking out the racetrack, in a sort of circle, the exact shape doesn't really matter."

20

The Dodo then placed all of them along the course and told them to start running when they liked and stop when they liked.

After they had been running for half an hour and were quite dry again, the Dodo suddenly called out, "The race is over!" And they all crowded round it, gasping and asking, "Who has won?"

This was a question the Dodo could not answer immediately. In fact it sat for a long time deep in thought. At last it said, "Everybody has won, and all must have prizes."

"But who is to give the prizes?" several of the animals cried, looking anxious.

"Why *she*, of course," said the Dodo, pointing to Alice, and the whole party at once crowded round Alice, calling out, "Prizes! Prizes!"

Poor Alice! She had no idea what to do, and in despair she pulled out of her pocket a box of colored candies which she remembered her big sister had given her. "Here you are," she said rather shyly. "There is one for each of you!"

"What about you?" the Mouse said suddenly. "You must have a prize!"

Alice shook her head. "I haven't anything else in my pocket – only a thimble!"

"Hand it over," said the Dodo. "Give it to me."

All the animals watched gravely. The Dodo bowed

and then solemnly presented the thimble to Alice, saying, "We beg you to accept this most handsome thimble." When it had finished this short speech, everyone cheered.

Alice thought it was all very silly but she did not dare laugh, though she wanted to very much. She bowed instead and thanked the Dodo.

The next thing was to eat the candy. Some of the big birds complained they could not even taste theirs.

Alice was surprised the Mouse did not complain. In fact, when she thought about it, she was quite surprised that the Mouse had joined the party. "It must have forgiven me," she decided.

The Mouse wanted to attract all the attention. It looked first at Alice and then at the Dodo. And the Dodo told everyone to sit in a ring. Then it turned to the Mouse and begged it to tell them a story.

"You could tell us something about yourself," said Alice. "Why you are so scared of you-know-what?" She broke off, not liking to mention the dreaded word CAT in case the Mouse rushed off again.

"Mine is a long, sad tale," said the Mouse, turning to Alice and sighing deeply.

"It is a long tail, certainly," said Alice. "I don't believe I have seen such a long tail."

"I am not talking about my *tail*," said the Mouse, beginning to look offended.

"Please don't take offense!" Alice cried, sitting down close to the Mouse and taking hold of its long tail. "You haven't even begun to tell us your story, and I'm sure we all want to hear it."

"I find you very stupid," exclaimed the Mouse, twisting round to glare at Alice out of bright little eyes. "And I'll ask you to let go of my tail this minute, if you please . . ."

"You won't run away, will you?" Alice asked.

But the Mouse only growled in reply and pulled its tail free. Then it got up and walked away.

"If I had my little cat, Dinah, here," Alice remarked, "she would soon fetch it back. She's a wizard at catching mice and little birds!" As she spoke everyone got to their feet and began hurrying away. Alice watched them go wishing she hadn't mentioned Dinah!

# Chapter 4
## THE RABBIT SENDS IN A LITTLE BILL

When all the animals had gone, poor Alice felt very lonely and she began to cry again. In a little while, however, she heard pattering of little feet and she looked up eagerly. It was the White Rabbit trotting towards her, even more splendidly dressed. She saw that it was looking very anxiously about as if it had lost something, and she heard it say,

"The Duchess! The Duchess! Oh, my dear paws! She'll have me executed as sure as ferrets are ferrets. Where *can* I have dropped them?"

Alice guessed it was looking for the fan and the white gloves.

It didn't take the White Rabbit long to notice Alice, and it called out to her in an angry voice.

"Mary Ann, now what are you doing here? Run home this moment and fetch me a pair of gloves and a fan and be quick about it!"

Alice was so frightened by the Rabbit's angry tone that she ran off at once in the direction it was pointing and very soon came upon a neat little house with a bright brass plate on the door.

As soon as she read the name *W. Rabbit* on the plate she went in without knocking and hurried upstairs, hoping she wouldn't meet the real Mary Ann and be turned away.

By the time she found her way into a tidy little room with a table by the window, she was beginning to feel ready for the next adventure. She picked up the fan and a pair of white kid gloves on the table, and was just about to leave the room when she saw a little bottle that stood near the looking-glass. Alice hesitated. Then she uncorked it and put it to her lips. "I do hope it makes me get bigger!" she thought. And so it did – sooner than she had expected! She had to lie down with one foot up the chimney and one arm out of the window.

"Curiouser and curiouser!" said Alice. "I wish I hadn't drunk so much . . ."

Just then she heard a voice outside. "Mary Ann," said the voice, "fetch me my gloves at once." And there came a pattering of little feet on the stairs.

When the Rabbit found it couldn't get in because the door was blocked by Alice,

she heard it mutter, "I'll have to get in by the window." "Oh, no you won't," she thought, and she suddenly spread out her hand and made a snatch in the air. There was a shriek and a fall and a crash of broken glass.

Next came an angry voice – the Rabbit's – "Pat! Pat! Where are you?"

"Sure I'm here, yer honour, digging . . ."

"Come and help me out of this cucumber frame," said the Rabbit crossly. "And tell Bill to fetch the ladder . . ."

"I don't like it . . ." Pat's voice was anxious.

Alice tried to pick up more words. There was more talk about ladders – two ladders now . . .

Then somebody said, "If you rope them together, they will be long enough to reach the chimney . . ." Another voice cried, "Now then, Bill, up you go!"

"So Bill's coming down the chimney!" she thought.

Alice waited for a moment to give Bill time to climb the ladder. When she heard a little animal scratching and scrambling almost above her, she gave one sharp kick up the chimney.

"So much for you, Bill!" she said aloud. "Whoever you are, I hope you won't hold it against me . . ."

There was a long silence and then suddenly a whole lot of voices. One, louder than the rest, Alice was sure she recognized. It was the White Rabbit's voice, she was sure of it.

"Watch out! Look where you're going!" it shouted. And then, "One of you stand by the hedge. Somebody bring up the barrow . . ."

There was another silence. Then Alice heard the
Rabbit shout, "Look, there he goes! There goes old
Bill! Now then – get ready to catch . . ."

"I hope old Bill had a soft landing," Alice said to
herself, as the sound of a feeble little squeaking voice
came to her. "No, no, no more brandy, if you please
. . . I don't know what happened . . . just something
came at me like – like a Jack-in-the-box, and up I goes
like a sky rocket . . ."

There was a sudden babble of voices and then the
Rabbit's loud and clear, "We'll burn down the house!"

"If you do!" Alice shouted, "I'll set Dinah at you!"

After a minute, she heard the Rabbit say, "We'll try the pebbles first . . ." And a shower of pebbles came in at the window, some hitting her in the face. Alice noticed with some surprise that they were all turning into cakes, and she swallowed one immediately.

To her delight she began shrinking at once, and as soon as she was small enough to get through the door, she ran out of the house. Outside she found a crowd of little animals and birds.

"There she is!" one of the party cried. "There goes the cause of all the trouble . . ."

Alice took shelter behind a big blue flower which she thought might be a kind of bluebell – a giant one – until she remembered how small she was. It was fortunate that just at the moment when they were trying to decide who should grab hold of her, the poor little lizard, Bill, began giving out pathetic squeaks. "Help! Help! It must be the shock . . ."

"Hold up, old fellow!" cried some of the party, and the two Guinea Pigs ran to him.

"Give him more of that brandy," somebody suggested, and the brandy bottle was immediately produced, and poor Bill spluttered and choked with every sip.

"So much for old Bill!" Alice thought. "Well, they all seem to have forgotten about me . . ." Without wasting any more time she turned her back on the group and ran off as fast as she could. To her delight she soon found herself in a thick wood where she decided she would be safe.

"The first thing I must do," said Alice to herself, as she wandered about in the wood, "is to grow to my right size again." While she was peering about the trees, she heard a sharp bark and then saw an enormous puppy looking at her with large eyes.

Alice dodged behind a great thistle to keep herself from being knocked over as the puppy made a dash at her. Then she threw a stick and while the puppy chased after it she made her escape.

Chapter 5

# ADVICE FROM A CATERPILLAR

Alice ran until she was quite tired and out of breath. When at last she stopped she leaned against a buttercup to rest herself. There was a large mushroom growing near her, very much bigger than herself, and when she stretched up on tiptoe and peeped over the edge, her eyes met those of a large blue caterpillar that was sitting on top quietly smoking a long hookah, and taking not the slightest notice of her or of anything else.

When at last the Caterpillar spoke it was in a slow, sleepy voice. "Who are you?" it asked.

"I'm not quite sure," Alice replied shyly. "Being so many different sizes in one day is very confusing, you know."

The Caterpillar puffed away at the hookah and then asked again, "Who are you?"

"I think you ought to tell me who you are," said Alice, feeling rather irritated. "That would be polite!" She was just going to turn away when the Caterpillar spoke again.

"Can you remember anything?" it asked. "Anything at all?"

The Caterpillar puffed away
for a time, then went on,
"Like – *You are old, Father
William!*" Alice put her hands
behind her back and began:

*"You are old, Father William," the young man said,*
  *"And your hair has become very white;*
*And yet you incessantly stand on your head –*
  *Do you think, at your age, it is right?"*

*"In my youth," Father William replied to his son,*
  *"I feared it might injure the brain;*
*But, now that I'm perfectly sure I have none,*
  *Why, I do it again and again."*

"You are old," said the youth,
   "as I mentioned before,
And have grown most uncommonly fat;
Yet you turned a back-somersault
     in at the door –
Pray, what is the reason of that?"

"In my youth," said the sage,
   as he shook his grey locks,
"I kept all my limbs very supple
By the use of this ointment –
    one shilling the box –
Allow me to sell you a couple?"

"You are old," said the youth,
   "and your jaws are too weak
For anything tougher than suet;
Yet you finished the goose,
    with the bones and the beak –
Pray, how did you manage to do it?"

"In my youth," said his father,
              "I took to the law,
And argued each case with my wife;
And the muscular strength,
             which it gave to my jaw,
Has lasted the rest of my life."

"You are old," said the youth,
            "one would hardly suppose
That your eye was as steady as ever;
Yet you balanced an eel
            on the end of your nose –
What made you so awfully clever?"

"I have answered three questions,
           and that is enough,"
Said his father; "don't give yourself airs!
Do you think I can listen
           all day to such stuff?
Be off, or I'll kick you downstairs!"

"That's not quite right," said the Caterpillar, when Alice came to a stop.

"I know," said Alice timidly. "Some of the words got changed . . ."

"Well, what size do you want to be?" the Caterpillar suddenly demanded. And, without waiting for a reply, it yawned once or twice and shook itself. Then it got down from the mushroom and began crawling away, merely remarking as it went, "One side will make you grow taller and the other side shorter."

Alice looked thoughtfully at the big
mushroom. Then she broke a bit off the
edge with each hand. A morsel from the
left hand sent her shooting upwards until
all she could see when she looked down was an
immense length of neck rising like a stalk out of a sea of
green leaves. She was just practicing bending her long
neck when a large pigeon flew at her, at the same time,
hissing, "Serpent! Serpent!"

"I'm not a serpent," said Alice, "I'm a girl, and if
you think I'm looking for eggs, I'm not!"

"Then be off," said the Pigeon, "this is my tree!"

Alice crouched down among the branches as well as she could until she remembered she still had a piece of mushroom in her right hand and began nibbling it carefully. Soon she had succeeded in bringing herself down to her usual height and she set off through the woods. After a time she came suddenly upon a little house. Alice saw at once that she was much too large to get into it.

"Whoever lives there," Alice thought, "will be frightened out of their wits if they see me this size!" And she began nibbling at the bit of mushroom in her right hand again until she considered she was the right size to go to the door and ask to be let in. "Well, whoever lives there is not going to mind me now," she told herself. "I'm the right size for their little house."

## Chapter 6

## PIG AND PEPPER

Alice was wondering if she should knock loudly or gently, when suddenly a footman in livery came running out of the wood. He rapped loudly at the door which was opened immediately by another footman in livery. The Fish-Footman produced a letter, nearly as big as himself. "For the Duchess," he said, "an invitation –

an invitation," he repeated, "from the Queen to play croquet." Then he bowed low to the Frog-Footman before running off. The Frog-Footman dropped the letter on the step, and Alice ventured to show herself.

"If you please," she began, "can you tell me how to get in? I very much want to . . ."

"There's certainly no use knocking," said the Footman. "They're making such a noise inside nobody could possibly hear you."

No doubt there was a most extraordinary noise going on within – a constant howling and sneezing.

By now the Footman was looking up
into the sky and Alice wondered why.
But just then the door of the house
opened, and a large blue plate came
skimming out, just missing the
Footman's head.

"Will you please tell me what to do?"
Alice began again.

"Anything you like," said the Footman.

"Then there's no use talking to you," said Alice, and she pushed open the door and went in.

The door led into a large kitchen which was full of smoke. The Duchess was sitting on a three-legged stool, nursing a baby. The cook was stirring a huge cauldron which seemed full of soup and PEPPER. Only the cook and the huge cat were not sneezing. Between sneezes, Alice managed to ask the Duchess why the cat was grinning from ear to ear.

"Because it's a Cheshire Cat, that's why," said the Duchess, and she began tossing the baby with such

violence that Alice cried, "Oh, please, watch what you're doing . . ." As she spoke, the cook started showering the Duchess with pans, plates and other cooking things.

"Here, you may nurse it a bit," the Duchess suddenly said, and she got up and flung the baby at Alice. The poor little thing was snorting like a steam-engine and was really looking very odd so Alice decided to take it outside.

Once outside, Alice looked
into its face to see if it was
crying. There was no doubt it
was changing. Its nose looked
more like a snout and its eyes
were getting extremely small.
She walked on a little way
with it in her arms before
saying, "If you're turning into
a pig, I really don't want
anything to do with you!"
And she put the little creature
down and watched it trot
away quietly into the wood.

Alice was a little startled
when she noticed the Cheshire
Cat sitting on the bough of the
tree. It was grinning at her in a
friendly way and she was just
about to ask it a simple
question when it vanished.
She waited patiently until it
reappeared. "Which way do
you think I ought to walk
now?" she asked rather shyly.

"It really doesn't matter which way you walk," said the Cat. "In one direction," it went on, waving its right paw, "lives a Hatter, and in the other, lives a March Hare. They're both mad!"

Alice set off in the direction of the March Hare's house and she had not gone far before she came in sight of it. "Somebody mad must live here," she told herself, as she stared at the ear-shaped chimneys and the roof thatched with real fur. "I've never in all my life seen such a funny house."

## Chapter 7

## A MAD TEA-PARTY

There was a table set out under a tree at the front of the house, and Alice began walking slowly towards it. She saw that the Hare and the Hatter were having tea. There was a Dormouse on the table between them and they were using it as a cushion.

The table was a large one, but the three were all crowded together at one corner of it, and when they

saw Alice they cried out, "No room! No room!"

"There's plenty of room," said Alice indignantly, and she sat down in a large armchair at one end of the table. "Have some wine," the March Hare said unexpectedly. Alice looked all round the table but there appeared to be only tea. "I don't see any wine," she said at last.

"There isn't any," said the March Hare. "Never was!" Before Alice could think of something to say in reply, the Hatter took a watch out of his pocket. "What day is it?" he asked. He shook the watch once or twice and then held it to his ear.

Alice thought a little and then said, "The fourth."

"Two days wrong," sighed the Hatter. "I told you butter wouldn't suit the works!" he added, looking very angry at the March Hare.

"It was the best butter," the March Hare meekly replied. And he took the watch and looked at it gloomily. Then he dipped it into his cup of tea, and looked at it again. But he could think of nothing better to say than repeat, "It was the *best* butter."

Alice had been staring at the watch. "What a funny watch!" she remarked at last. "It tells the day of the month, and doesn't tell what time it is!"

"Why should it?" muttered the Hatter. "Does your watch tell you what year it is?"

"Of course not," replied Alice, and fell silent.

"Exactly," said the Hatter. And he too fell silent.

Alice sat back in her chair and waited to see what would happen next. Presently the Hatter said, "The Dormouse is asleep again!" And he poured a little warm tea on its nose.

"I agree with everything you say!" the Dormouse squeaked without opening its eyes.

"Six o'clock and storytime!" the Hatter suddenly cried. And he began waving his teaspoon until it finally pointed at the Dormouse.

"Your turn," the Hatter said.

The Dormouse slowly opened
its eyes, "Once upon a time," it
began, "there were three little
sisters, and they lived at the
bottom of a well . . ."

"What did they live on?" Alice
asked, with great interest.

"They lived on molasses,"
said the Dormouse. "In fact it
was a molasses-well . . ."

"They couldn't!" Alice began.

"Don't talk so much," said the
Hatter, "Keep quiet . . ."

This remark so annoyed
Alice that she got up and left the
table just as they were putting
the Dormouse into the teapot.
As she picked her way through
the wood she noticed that one
of the trees had a door leading
right into it. "I might as well go
in," Alice thought.
And in she went.

# Chapter 8

## THE QUEEN'S CROQUET GROUND

Once more Alice found herself in the long hall, and close to the little glass table. "I'll manage things better now," she thought, taking the little golden key and unlocking the tiny door. Then she nibbled at the piece of mushroom she had kept. When she was about a foot high, she walked down the little passage, and found herself at last in the beautiful garden.

A large rose-tree stood near the entrance. The roses on it were white, but they were being painted red by three busy gardeners.

Suddenly a shout went up, "The King and
Queen of Hearts!" And Alice watched the
Royal Procession go by, splendidly

decorated with clubs, diamonds
and spades, and the ten royal
children ornamented with hearts.

Alice thought the Rabbit might notice her but he didn't seem to though the Queen most certainly did. "Who is this?" she demanded. "Who are you, child?"

"I'm Alice, so please your Majesty," said Alice.

The Queen then turned her attention to the three gardeners who had not completed their painting. "Off with their heads!" she screamed.

"That's not fair," said Alice, and she put the poor gardeners into a large flowerpot that stood near.

The procession moved on until the
Queen shouted "Croquet time!" And
Alice was given a flamingo for a mallet.
The balls were live hedgehogs.

Alice looked round for the White Rabbit who had appeared so unexpectedly at her side but he had vanished. Meantime she was struggling with the flamingo, which would twist itself round every now and then and look into her face. The other players were all shouting and quarreling, and the Queen was now in a furious passion. She was stamping about, shouting, "Off with his head!" or "Off with her head!"

Alice began to feel very uneasy about her own head!

She was looking around for some way of escape when she saw a curious appearance in the air. It puzzled her at first, but after a minute she made it out to be a grin, and she said to herself, "It must be the Cheshire Cat!"

In another minute the whole head appeared and Alice began telling it all about the game. "There aren't any rules," she said, "and the Queen's hedgehog always runs away when it sees mine coming. If you ask me it's all very silly."

Alice broke off as the King came up. "Who are you talking to?" he asked, staring up at the Cat's head.

"It's a friend – a Cheshire Cat," said Alice.

"Well, I don't like the look of it," said the King.

"Off with his head," shouted the Queen, when the King asked her to have the Cat removed.

"I'll get the executioner myself," said the King eagerly, and he hurried off.

A small crowd had gathered when he returned with the executioner, who was looking very grim. "I can't cut off a head unless it is fixed on to a body," he said over and over again, despite loud shouts of "Silence!" from the Queen.

At last someone suggested asking the Duchess.

"Get her!" said the Queen. "She's in prison." But before the Duchess arrived, the Cat had gone.

# Chapter 9

## THE MOCK TURTLE'S STORY

As soon as the Duchess arrived, she went straight up to Alice and tucked her arm affectionately into hers.

"Glad to see you, old thing!" she cried.

Alice was relieved to find her in such a pleasant temper. "It must have been all that pepper in her kitchen," she told herself, as the Duchess went on squeezing her arm with great affection.

"I dare say you are wishing I'd put my arm round your waist," said the Duchess presently. "But I am doubtful about the temper of your flamingo."

Here, to Alice's surprise, the Duchess fell silent and Alice looked up to find the Queen in front of them, frowning like a thunderstorm.

"A fine day, your Majesty," the Duchess began, in a low, weak voice.

"Now I give fair warning," shouted the Queen, taking a firm hold of her flamingo,

"either you or your head must be off, and that in about half–no–time! Take your choice."

The Duchess looked very alarmed. Then, without even as much as a goodbye to Alice, she was gone in a flash.

"Let's get on with the game," the Queen said to Alice, who was much too frightened to say a word except for, "Very well, your Majesty! Anything you say!"

"Follow me to the croquet ground," commanded the Queen, and Alice obeyed.

By the end of half an hour
all the players were under
sentence of execution, and the
Queen, suddenly turning to
Alice, asked if she had seen the
Mock Turtle yet.

"No," said Alice, "I don't
even know what a Mock
Turtle is."

"Come on, then," said the
Queen. "He'll tell you his story."

They soon came upon a
Gryphon asleep in the sun,
and the Queen shouted at it,
"Up lazy thing!"

The Gryphon opened its eyes and the Queen continued, "Take this young lady to see the Mock Turtle. I must go back and see to all the executions I have ordered."

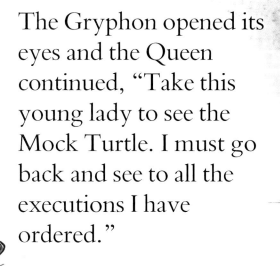

"Come on," said the Gryphon, getting to its feet, and Alice went slowly after it until they came upon the Mock Turtle, who looked at them with large eyes full of tears but said nothing.

"This here young lady," said the Gryphon, pushing Alice forward, "wants to hear your story, she do. And that's a fact!"

"I'll tell it to her," said the Mock Turtle, in a deep, hollow voice. "Sit down, both of you and don't speak a word until I have finished."

So they sat down and nobody spoke for some minutes. Alice waited patiently until the Mock Turtle, with a deep sigh, said, "Once I was a real Turtle . . ." These words were followed by another silence and heavy sobbing on the part of the Turtle. Then he went on, "When we were little we went to school in the sea, though you might doubt it."

"I don't doubt it at all," interrupted Alice. "I never said I did!"

"Yes, you did," said the Turtle.

"Hold your tongue," the Gryphon said to Alice, and the Mock Turtle went on, "We had the very best education. In fact we went to school every day."

"I go to school every day," said Alice. "You needn't be so proud as all that . . ."

"Do – do you have extras – like French and – and music lessons?"

"Yes," said Alice, "we learn French and music."

"And washing?" said the Mock Turtle.

"Certainly not!" said Alice indignantly.

"Ah! Then yours wasn't a really good school," said the Mock Turtle in a tone of great relief. "Now at ours, they had French, music *and* washing – as an extra. Washing was special!"

The Mock Turtle was slowly becoming more cheerful, and he began to describe his learned teacher with a great deal of feeling. "He never took lessons without a pointer in one flipper and a book in the other," he said enthusiastically.

Alice was not sure if she dare interrupt again, but when the Mock Turtle stopped to do some breathing exercises, she said, "Do tell me about other lessons you had to learn under the sea . . ."

"That's enough about lessons," cried the Gryphon. "Tell her about the games!"

Chapter 10

# THE LOBSTER QUADRILLE

The Mock Turtle sighed deeply, and drew the back of one flipper across his eyes. Then he said, "You have no idea what a Lobster Quadrille is?"

"Show me," said Alice. And the two creatures immediately began jumping about like mad things in front of her.

"It must be a very pretty dance," Alice ventured after a time, when the dancers suddenly sat down.

"It is," said the Mock Turtle. "Everybody joins in."

"That's right," said the Gryphon, very much out of breath.

"They form two lines," cried the Mock Turtle. "Seals, turtles, crabs, snails, big fishes and very little ones . . ."

"Some with a lobster as a

partner," interrupted the Gryphon. "The lobsters are ever so important . . ."

"I expect they are," said Alice. "It must be exciting."

"The lobsters get tossed about a bit, of course," said the Mock Turtle. "The sea gets so crowded . . ."

"What about the music?" Alice asked. "Do you have any?"

"I sing," said the Mock Turtle, in a low, sad voice.

"I know some verses about an owl and a panther eating a pie," said Alice, standing up. "And there's a verse about a lobster. It begins, 'Tis the voice of the Lobster . . .'"

"What did the panther do?" asked the Mock Turtle.

"It ate the piecrust and the meat and the gravy," said Alice. "The poor little owl didn't get . . ." she broke off as a cry was heard in the distance, "The trial's just beginning!"

"Come on," cried the Gryphon, taking Alice by the hand. "We must hurry!"

# Chapter 11
# WHO STOLE THE TARTS?

Alice found it quite hard to keep up with the Gryphon, but it kept a firm hold of her hand and she had no choice.

They soon caught up with a great crowd hurrying along.

"I suppose all these people and the little animals are going to the trial?" Alice managed to gasp. "I suppose it's being held in a court? I happen to know that is where trials are held."

"You suppose right," said the Gryphon in a deep voice.

The King and Queen of Hearts were already seated on their throne when they arrived.

The Knave was standing before them, in chains, with a soldier on each side to guard him. Near the King was the White Rabbit, with a trumpet in one hand.

"The White Rabbit must be the Herald," Alice decided. "That's why he has the trumpet and the scroll."

Then she noticed the King had his crown over the wig. "He's going to act as the judge," she thought, pleased she knew so much about courts.

"I read about courts of justice in a book," she told the Gryphon, who was standing quite close. "That's the jury box over there, and those twelve creatures must be the jurors . . ." She repeated the last word several times being rather proud of it, but the Gryphon made no comment.

"I suppose that large dish of tarts on the table is the evidence," Alice went on, after a short silence. "I wish they'd get the trial done and pass them round afterwards as refreshments. They certainly look good enough to eat!"

"Talk in a whisper," said the Gryphon, "if you must!"

Alice was about to protest at the Gryphon's unkind tone when suddenly the King cried, "Herald, read the accusation!"

On this the White Rabbit blew three blasts on the trumpet and then unrolled the parchment scroll, and read:

*"The Queen of Hearts,*
  *she made some tarts,*
*All on a summer day.*

*The Knave of Hearts,*
  *he stole those tarts,*
*And took them quite away!"*

"Call the first witness," said the King, and the White Rabbit blew three blasts on the trumpet, and called out, "First Witness!" The first witness was the Hatter. He came in with a teacup in one hand and a piece of bread and butter in the other.

"I beg your pardon, your Majesty," he began, "for not finishing my tea when I was sent for."

"You ought to have finished your tea," said the King severely. "Give your evidence."

The poor Hatter trembled so much that he shook both his shoes off. "I c–can't remember about the t–teaparty or the t–tarts," he said miserably.

"You are a very poor speaker," said the King frowning. "You may stand down . . ."

"And take his head off outside," the Queen told one of the officers, but the Hatter was out of sight before the officer could get to the door.

"Call the next witness," said the King.

The next witness was the Duchess's cook. She carried the pepper-pot in her hand, and the people near the door began sneezing as soon as she appeared. "Give your evidence," said the King.

"Shan't," said the cook.

The King looked anxiously at the White Rabbit, who said in a low voice, "Your Majesty must cross-examine this witness . . ."

"Well, if I must I must," said the King in a deep voice. "What are the tarts made of?"

"Pepper, mostly," said the cook.

The Queen looked at the cook through her lorgnette, and Alice couldn't help thinking that the cook would soon be losing her head if she wasn't more polite. All at once a sleepy voice from behind cried, "Molasses!"

"Off with his head!" shrieked the Queen. As the Dormouse was dragged away, the cook made her escape.

"Call the next witness," the King said, pleased that the cook had gone.

# Chapter 12

## ALICE'S EVIDENCE

At the top of his shrill little voice the White Rabbit read out the name, "Alice!"

"Here!" cried Alice, quite forgetting that she had been growing bigger and bigger in the last few minutes. And she jumped up in such a hurry that she tipped over the jury box with the edge of her skirt.

All the jurymen were upset and some fell on the heads of the crowd below, while others sprawled about on the ground.

Seeing the horror on the White Rabbit's face, Alice stammered, "Oh, I do beg your pardon! Let me help to put them back!" And she began picking up some of the poor little jurymen and trying, without much success, to fit them into the jury box. Somehow, she had a vague idea that they must all be collected at once or they would die. "I must be thinking of the time I upset the goldfish bowl and nearly let the goldfish die," she told herself, watching an angry bluebird zooming down on a defenceless duck. "Oh dear, I wish now I hadn't started growing again, I really do!"

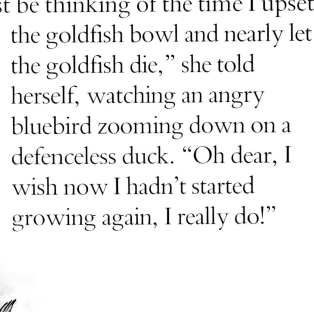

"The trial cannot proceed," said the King in a very serious voice, "until all the jurymen are back in their proper place – *all!*" he repeated, looking hard at Alice as he spoke.

Alice studied the jury box and saw that, in her haste, she had put the Lizard in head downwards, and the poor little thing was waving its tail about in a very pathetic way, being quite unable to move. She soon got it out again and put it right.

The King waited patiently until Alice had arranged the jurymen in their proper places and made sure they all had their slates and pencils. Most of them seemed to recover quickly from their upset except the Lizard, who just sat with its mouth open, gazing upwards.

"The trial may now proceed," said the King in the same serious voice, looking at Alice.

Alice stepped into the witness box, and the King said, "What do you know about this business?"

"Nothing," said Alice. "Nothing whatever!"

"That's very important," the King said, turning to the jury. They were just beginning to write this down on their slates, when the White Rabbit interrupted, "UNimportant, your Majesty means, of course," he said in a very respectful tone, but frowning and making faces at him as he spoke.

"UNimportant, of course, I mean," the King said quickly. "UNimportant, of course!" And he coughed.

Alice saw that some of the jury wrote 'important', and some wrote 'unimportant'.

Except for the poor little Lizard, all the jurymen were clearly waiting for the King to say something more. Instead he got out his notebook and after studying it for some time said, "Rule forty-two: *All persons more than a mile high to leave the court.*"

At this the White Rabbit jumped up in a great hurry. "This paper has just been picked up, your Majesty," he cried. "I haven't opened it, but it seems to be a letter written by the prisoner to somebody!"

"It must have been that!" exclaimed the King, "unless it was written to *nobody*. Who is it sent to?"

The White Rabbit unfolded the paper. "It isn't a letter, after all, your Majesty, it's some verses."

"Please, your Majesty," said the Knave suddenly, "I didn't write it, and they can't prove I did."

And he got down on one knee, despite his chains, before adding, "Besides there's no name signed at the end of it so that proves it . . ."

"That proves nothing," said the King. "Nothing whatsoever!"

At this there was a general clapping of hands, and the King went on, "You must have meant some mischief, Knave, or you would have signed it."

"That proves his guilt!" cried the Queen.

"It proves nothing of the sort!" Alice shouted. "You don't know what the verses are about . . ."

"Read them," said the King. And the White Rabbit put on his glasses and began to read. But he read so fast and the verses were so strange that even the jury stopped writing anything down on their slates. And the Queen threw an inkpot at poor little Lizard Bill who had not managed to write anything on his slate that made sense which wasn't really very surprising!

"It's all stuff and nonsense!" Alice cried. "If the Knave had stolen the tarts he would have eaten them . . ."

"Hold your tongue," said the Queen, turning purple with rage.

"I won't," said Alice.

"Off with her head!" shouted the Queen.

"Who cares for you?" said Alice. "You're nothing but a pack of cards!"

At this the whole pack rose up in the air and came flying down on her. Alice gave a little scream and tried to beat them off, and found herself lying on the bank with her sister gently brushing away some dead leaves that had fluttered down from the trees on to her face.

"Wake up, Alice dear," said her sister. "What a long sleep you've had!"

"Oh, I've had such a curious dream!" said Alice. "Such a wonderful dream! Do let me tell you about it!"

## The End